Green MANOR

I

Assassins and Gentlemen

Illustrated by: Denis Bodart
Written by: Fabien Vehlmann

CINEBOOK
EXPRESSO

Original title: Green Manor 1 – Assassins et gentlemen

Original edition: © Dupuis, 2005 by Vehlmann & Bodart
www.dupuis.com
All rights reserved

English translation: © 2008 Cinebook Ltd

Translator: Elaine Kemp
Lettering and text layout: Imadjinn sarl
Printed in Spain by Just Colour Graphic

This edition first published in Great Britain in 2008 by
CINEBOOK Ltd
56 Beech Avenue
Canterbury, Kent
CT4 7TA
www.cinebook.com

A CIP catalogue record for this book
is available from the British Library

ISBN 978-1-905460-53-3

CINEBOOK
EXPRESSO

LONDON, BETHLEHEM PSYCHIATRIC HOSPITAL, 1899.

AH, DOCTOR THORNE, I'M VERY HAPPY TO MAKE YOUR ACQUAINTANCE!

I HAVE READ WITH CLOSE ATTENTION YOUR RECENT WORK ON INSANITY. BRILLIANT! I IMAGINE THAT YOU HAVE COME HERE TO STUDY ONE OF MY CHARGES?

IN FACT, I AM INTERESTED IN THE CASE OF THOMAS BELOW. I READ IN THE PRESS THAT HE HAD BEEN CONFINED IN YOUR ESTABLISHMENT.

AH—YES. A VERY STRANGE PERSON!

HE HAS WORKED ALL HIS LIFE AS A DOMESTIC SERVANT AT THE GREEN MANOR CLUB, WHERE HIS WORK HAS ALWAYS BEEN IRREPROACHABLE... UNTIL THIS VIOLENT FIT OF DEMENTIA STRUCK HIM A FEW DAYS BEFORE HIS RETIREMENT...

... HE THREATENED SEVERAL PEOPLE WITH A KITCHEN KNIFE.

MM..."SERIOUS PERSONALITY PROBLEMS, MORBID TENDENCIES, DELUSIONS OF PERSECUTION"... I AM ANXIOUS TO MEET HIM!

A GUARD WILL TAKE YOU TO HIS CELL.

HOWEVER, BEFORE I LEAVE YOU, WILL YOU ALLOW ME TO GIVE YOU SOME ADVICE?...

HE IS USUALLY QUITE CALM ... BUT BE ON YOUR GUARD!

4

SQUEAK
SQUEAK

CALL ME IF THERE IS ANY PROBLEM.

SQUEAK
SQUEAK

WELCOME TO THE CLUB, SIR!

HELLO, MR BELOW, HOW ARE YOU DOING?

I FEEL VERY TIRED. I AM ALMOST ONE HUNDRED YEARS OLD, YOU KNOW.

...YES, I AM A MANOR OF NEARLY A HUNDRED BUT WITH CREAKING BONES LIKE THE RIGGING OF AN OLD SAILING BOAT... THE DRAUGHTS PIERCE ME. I'M FREEZING!

A MANOR?... ARE YOU TALKING ABOUT THE CLUB WHERE YOU WORKED?

B.

5

THE GREEN MANOR CLUB, YES...

I AM THE SOUL OF THAT GREAT HOUSE...

...A GHOSTLY PHANTOM, I ATTENDED TO EVERYTHING.

MY WALLS HAVE BEEN WITNESS TO ALL THE WEIRD, RIDICULOUS OR SORDID HAPPENINGS...I HAVE SEEN SO MANY SHATTERED DESTINIES!

...AND ALL THE SPILT BLOOD! TAKE A GOOD LOOK AT MY FLOORS. THEY WILL HAVE TO BE RE-LAID.

WHAT IS IT YOU WANT TO SAY? WHAT "SHATTERED DESTINIES" DO YOU WANT TO TALK ABOUT?

YOU WISH TO KNOW MORE? THEN IT IS NECESSARY TO GET INTO THE CLUB, SIR. YOU COULD WITNESS THE SINISTER EVENTS FOR WHICH I HAVE BEEN THE SETTING.

PLEASE FOLLOW ME. WE'LL GO INTO THE GRAND SALON.

IT IS ALWAYS THERE THAT EVERYTHING STARTED.

c

Green MANOR

Delicious Shivers

GREEN MANOR CLUB, OCTOBER 1879.

GENTLEMEN! THIS IS THE EVENING ON WHICH DOCTOR BYRON IS COMING TO PROPOSE THE SUBJECT OF OUR DISCUSSION.

I REALLY BELIEVE THAT THIS MAY BE THE POOR OLD CHAP'S LAST CHAT.

GENTLEMEN, I WILL BE BRIEF. DO YOU BELIEVE THAT THERE CAN BE A MURDER WITHOUT A VICTIM AND WITHOUT A MURDERER?...

WHAT A STRANGE QUESTION!

WELL, BELIEVE IT OR NOT, SOMEONE IN FACT TOLD ME ABOUT A MURDER WITHOUT A VICTIM.

TELL US ABOUT IT, SIR FOSWELL!

WELL, THE AFFAIR HAPPENED AT THE BEGINNING OF THE CENTURY WHEN A YOUNG ARISTOCRAT, AGAINST THE ADVICE OF HIS PARENTS, MARRIED A PENNILESS ORPHAN GIRL.

ONE WEEK OF THIS CLANDESTINE PASSION WAS ENOUGH FOR THESE LOVEBIRDS TO UNDERSTAND HOW DIFFERENT THEIR WORLDS WERE.

SHE REFUSED TO MEET THE PEOPLE CLOSE TO HIM, AND HE TO MIX WITH HIS WIFE'S FRIENDS...

THEN, ONE NIGHT, IN THE COURSE OF A VIOLENT DISPUTE...

CRACK!

SPLASH!

REALISING WHAT HE HAD JUST DONE, THE YOUNG MAN WENT TO SEE HIS PARENTS TO APOLOGISE FOR HIS SHAMEFUL CONDUCT.

THEN HE WENT TO TURN HIMSELF IN TO THE POLICE, AS ANY REAL GENTLEMAN MUST DO IN SUCH A SITUATION.

A GENTLEMAN DOES NOT KILL HIS WIFE!

A GENTLEMAN REMAINS CELIBATE!

WHILE THE INVESTIGATION WAS TAKING PLACE, IT WAS IMPOSSIBLE FOR THE YOUNG MAN TO PROVE THAT THERE HAD BEEN A MURDER, AS THE BODY COULD NOT BE FOUND.

BUT ABOVE ALL, IT WAS IMPOSSIBLE FOR HIM TO PROVE THAT HE HAD BEEN MARRIED! THE LOCAL CLERGYMAN DENIED EVER HAVING SEEN HIM, AND HIS WIFE'S FRIENDS HAD ALL LEFT TOWN.

IT WAS EXPLAINED TO THE POLICE THAT THE YOUNG MAN HAD SOMETIMES BEEN SUBJECTED TO MILD BOUTS OF DEMENTIA...SO HE WAS RELEASED.

HE UNDERSTOOD THAT THE EXISTENCE OF HIS WIFE HAD BEEN EFFACED BY BOTTLES OF WINE AND DEATH THREATS. HIS FAMILY WAS VERY POWERFUL.

GIN · OLD TOM · ALES

HE MARRIED AGAIN, WITH A WOMAN OF HIS OWN SOCIAL CLASS, AND ONLY REVEALED THE AFFAIR ON HIS DEATHBED.

YES, BUT THAT ISN'T A MURDER WITHOUT A VICTIM...

2

IN FACT, THERE HAD BEEN A VICTIM, ALTHOUGH THE POLICE HAD NO KNOWLEDGE OF IT.

FOR MY PART, I ONCE HAD TO DEAL WITH A CASE OF MURDER WITHOUT A MURDERER.

TELL US ABOUT IT, INSPECTOR DARCROFT.

SIR THOMAS JOHNS, HAVING NO DESCENDANTS, HAD SUMMONED ALL HIS CLOSEST FRIENDS IN ORDER TO DRAW UP HIS WILL.

SUDDENLY, THE GROUP OF FRIENDS HEARD SIR THOMAS SHOUTING IN HIS OFFICE...

YOU WON'T GET AWAY WITH THIS, YOU FILTHY LITTLE WRETCH!!

BANG!

IT'S LOCKED FROM THE INSIDE!

KRAK

THE MURDER WEAPON, SIR THOMAS'S OWN GUN, WAS FOUND A FEW METRES FROM THE BODY.

THE WINDOWS WERE LOCKED AND THERE WAS NO FIREPLACE... NEVERTHELESS, THERE WAS NO TRACE OF THE ASSASSIN. IT WASN'T MORE THAN A FEW SECONDS FROM THE SHOT TO THE OPENING OF THE DOOR.

3

ONE MEMBER OF THE GROUP WAS SURE THAT HE HAD SEEN SOMEONE RUNNING IN THE GROUNDS, BUT THERE WAS NOTHING TO CONFIRM HIS STORY.

THE AUTOPSY REVEALED THAT THE SHOT HAD BEEN FIRED ABOUT ONE METRE FROM THE VICTIM. THUS, IT COULD NOT HAVE BEEN SUICIDE.

WHO HAD KILLED SIR THOMAS? NONE OF HIS FRIENDS HAD ANY INTEREST IN HIS PREMATURE DEATH, WHICH HAD DEPRIVED THEM OF THEIR INHERITANCE...BUT, ABOVE ALL, HOW HAD THE MURDER BEEN POSSIBLE?

THE ANSWER TO THIS MYSTERY WAS FOUND BY CHANCE SEVERAL WEEKS LATER...

WE HAD ARRESTED A YOUNG GYPSY FOR THEFT, AND SUDDENLY HE BEGAN TO TALK ABOUT "THE OLD MAN," SAYING "IT WASN'T HIS FAULT"...

HE TOLD US THAT HE OFTEN WENT INTO THE GROUNDS OF SIR THOMAS'S HOUSE AND THAT THE OLD MAN HAD SEVERAL TIMES THREATENED HIM WITH DEATH.

ON THE EVENING OF THE MURDER, HE HAD COME TO THE WINDOW OF SIR THOMAS'S OFFICE.

YOU WON'T GET AWAY WITH THIS, YOU FILTHY LITTLE WRETCH!!

4

CLICK

BANG

THUS, IT WAS AN UNFORTUNATE ACCIDENT INADVERTENTLY CAUSED BY THE YOUNG THIEF.

SOME TIME LATER, THE GYPSY WAS FOUND DEAD. NO DOUBT, THE FRIENDS OF SIR THOMAS HAD NOT FORGIVEN HIM FOR DOING THEM OUT OF THEIR INHERITANCE!

HO! HO! HA! HA! HA! HO! HO! HO! HO! HO! HO! HA! HA

THAT'S NO GOOD... SIR THOMAS WAS THE VICTIM OF A FORTUITOUS ACCIDENT, NOT OF A "MURDER WITHOUT A MURDERER."

I THINK WE HAVE TO RECOGNISE OUR INABILITY TO ANSWER DR BYRON'S QUESTION IN THE AFFIRMATIVE.

MURDER BEING BY DEFINITION THE ACTION OF AN INDIVIDUAL TO KILL ANOTHER INDIVIDUAL, ONE CANNOT HAVE A MURDER WITHOUT A VICTIM OR A MURDERER.

THERE EXISTS, HOWEVER, A CASE OF A MURDER WITHOUT MURDERER OR VICTIM...

DO YOU KNOW THE VENENUM ATTERMINATUM ATTEMPERATUM?

THE POISON OF THE BORGIAS...

WHICH WAS SURE TO KILL AND ON A DATE CHOSEN BY THE POISONER, SOMETIMES YEARS AFTER ITS INGESTION.

THERE WAS NO KNOWN ANTIDOTE.

THE RECIPE FOR THIS POISON IS COMPLETELY LOST.

IT IS NOT LOST FOR EVERYBODY, BECAUSE I POURED SOME OF THIS POISON INTO YOUR GLASSES LAST WEEK.

!!?

??!

ADMIT IT! FOR THE MOMENT NO MURDERER, NO VICTIM, BECAUSE YOU ARE ALL STILL LIVING.

HOWEVER, YOU HAVE ALREADY INGESTED THE POISON, SO I HAVE ACTUALLY COMMITTED A MURDER.

SUPPOSING WE AGREE TO CREDIT THIS BAD JOKE, WHAT WOULD BE YOUR MOTIVE?

YOUR INSUFFERABLE ARROGANCE... THE UNHEALTHY PLEASURE WITH WHICH YOU DISSECT HUMAN DRAMAS, ONLY TO GIVE YOURSELVES DELICIOUS SHIVERS.

I HAVE THEREFORE POURED A PERSONALISED DOSE OF POISON FOR EVERYONE!

YOU WILL DIE, ONE AFTER THE OTHER, ON THE DATES THAT I HAVE SET ACCORDING TO THE OPINION I HAVE OF EACH OF YOU.

THOSE FOR WHOM I HAVE THE LEAST REPUGNANCE WILL DIE LATER. I BID YOU GOODNIGHT.

OF COURSE HE WAS LYING... IT WOULD BE RIDICULOUS TO BELIEVE FOR A SINGLE SECOND...

BUT, ALREADY, WE WERE TRYING FEVERISHLY TO REMEMBER EVERYTHING THAT WE MIGHT HAVE SAID IN HIS PRESENCE.

ALL THE SUBJECTS FROM WHICH HE WOULD HAVE BEEN ABLE TO CHOOSE TO CONDEMN US.

IN THE IMPROBABLE CASE THAT HE HAD SPOKEN THE TRUTH, HOW MUCH TIME HAD HE ALLOWED EACH ONE?

FROM THAT DAY, THE DOUBT COMMENCED TO GNAW AT US MORE EFFECTIVELY THAN ANY POISON, KILLING US SLOWLY BUT SURELY.

TO SUM UP, A PERFECT MURDER. WITHOUT A VICTIM OR A MURDERER.

FOR THE MOMENT...

POST-SCRIPTUM

1ST AUGUST 1882 AT THE GREEN MANOR CLUB.

YOU HAVE MADE GREAT EFFORTS THIS TIME, DETECTIVE JOHNSON!

I CANNOT TAKE MUCH CREDIT. A LITTLE COMMON SENSE IS ENOUGH...

ALL THE SAME! TO ARREST THE BUTCHER OF WESTMINSTER!

ALL THE PAPERS ARE TALKING ABOUT YOUR EXPLOIT!

YOU HAVE EVEN BECOME THE DARLING OF ALL THE LADIES!

I ALWAYS THOUGHT THAT THE MURDERER WAS A WELSHMAN.

ALL THIS FUSS BORES ME. BRING ME A SCOTCH TO THE SMALL SALON.

FOR MY PART, I FIND YOUR REPUTATION QUITE EXAGGERATED.

TIMES
DETECTIVE JOHNSON PUTS WESTMINSTER BUTCHER UUDER LOCK AND KEY

ARRESTING A FEEBLE-MINDED BRUTE DOES NOT SEEM TO ME TO DESERVE SUCH EULOGIES.

THE "FEEBLE-MINDED BRUTE" THWARTED SCOTLAND YARD FOR A MONTH.

HA! HA! TO SUCCEED IN SUCH A "TOUR DE FORCE," A CRIMINAL ONLY HAS TO AVOID GIVING HIMSELF UP!

SIR, I DO NOT KNOW YOU AND I WILL NOT LISTEN TO YOU ANY LONGER.

MY NAME IS SIR ALFRED MONTGOMERY, AND I PROPOSE A CHALLENGE.

TOMORROW EVENING, AT MIDNIGHT, I WILL KILL PRETTY MRS ROWE WHO LIVES AT 15 GRAFTON STREET. THE QUESTION IS WHETHER YOU ARE CAPABLE OF PREVENTING THIS MURDER.

ARE YOU MAD?!

THE RULES ARE AS FOLLOWS:

PRIMO, IF YOU BREATHE A WORD OF THIS AFFAIR, I WILL DENY HAVING THIS CONVERSATION AND I WILL SUE YOU FOR LIBEL.

SECUNDO, IF YOU ASK FOR HELP FROM SCOTLAND YARD, EVEN WITHOUT GIVING MY NAME, I WILL CONSIDER THAT YOU HAVE LOST...

...AND THAT YOUR REPUTATION IS INDEED OVERRATED.

AH, YES... AND TERTIO...

IF YOU DO NOT SUCCEED IN SAVING MRS ROWE, YOU ALSO WILL DIE.

HE HAS DARED TO TAUNT ME WHILE GIVING ME THE DATE AND HOUR OF THE CRIME!!

2

I'M GOING TO PAY THIS MONTGOMERY BACK FOR HIS ARROGANCE!

YOUR IRREGULARS ARE HERE, SIR.

WHAT HAVE YOU FOUND OUT ABOUT MRS ROWE?

A PRETTY LITTLE THING! HER HUSBAND DEPARTED YESTERDAY ON A BUSINESS TRIP. APART FROM ONE SERVANT, SHE IS ALONE IN THAT BIG HOUSE.

AN IDEAL PREY. AND WHAT ABOUT SIR ALFRED?

HE IS A LAWYER WHO HARDLY EVER GOES OUT AND LEADS A VERY BORING LIFE.

MM... HE IS CRAFTY AND WILL NOT MAKE ANY FALSE MOVES. HE HAS IT ALL PLANNED OUT.

ALL THE SAME, YOU WILL GO AND WATCH HIS EVERY ACTION AND GESTURE... THE OTHER IRREGULARS COME WITH ME.

SOMEONE WANTS TO KILL ME TONIGHT?!

IT IS FORBIDDEN FOR ME TO TELL YOU ANY MORE AT THE MOMENT... BUT I BEG YOU TO BELIEVE ME, AS INCREDIBLE AS IT MAY SEEM.

DETECTIVE JOHNSON, YOUR REPUTATION IS ENOUGH. I PLACE MYSELF IN YOUR HANDS.

YOUR SERVANT. IS SHE A RELIABLE PERSON?

DO YOU THINK THAT SHE COULD...? MY GOD... I'M GOING TO GIVE HER THE EVENING OFF.

WILL YOU PERMIT ME TO HAVE A LOOK IN YOUR BEDROOM?

IF IT IS REALLY NECESSARY...

GOOD. IF IT'S NOT INCONVENIENT TO YOU, I WILL POSITION MYSELF OUTSIDE YOUR DOOR.

MY GOD, ALL THIS SEEMS SO UNREAL!

DON'T WORRY, MRS ROWE; MY IRREGULARS ARE ON WATCH ALL AROUND YOUR HOUSE AND WILL WHISTLE AT THE LEAST SUSPICIOUS MOVEMENT.

DON'T HESITATE TO CALL ME IF YOU HAVE THE SLIGHTEST PROBLEM.

I WON'T FAIL TO DO THAT.

4

FIVE MINUTES TO MIDNIGHT... SIR ALFRED APPEARED SO SURE OF HIMSELF... WHAT DID HE HAVE IN THE BACK OF HIS MIND?

THE BEDROOM... HE MUST HAVE THOUGHT OF SOME SORT OF MACHIAVELLIAN TRICK TO ENTER MRS ROWE'S BEDROOM...

KNOCK KNOCK

I THINK IT MIGHT BE SAFER IF I MOUNT GUARD INSIDE YOUR BEDROOM.

TO TELL THE TRUTH, I DIDN'T DARE TO ASK YOU!

I WILL POST MYSELF HERE.

I MUST THANK YOU AGAIN FOR YOUR COURAGE.

I'M ONLY DOING MY DUTY, MADAME.

SHOULD WE STOP HIM?

IT'S MR ROWE! WE CAN HARDLY PREVENT HIM FROM ENTERING HIS OWN HOME!

MY GOD, IT'S MY HUSBAND. GO QUICKLY! IF HE EVER LEARNS ABOUT THE LETTER!...

WHAT LETTER?

EPILOGUE...

MR MONTGOMERY?

I AM VERY SORRY TO TROUBLE YOU...

WELL, OUT WITH IT, MY BOY.

ER...

WELL, I WAS A FRIEND OF DETECTIVE JOHNSON.

WE ARE ALL DEEPLY SORRY ABOUT HIS DEATH.

WELL, HE ASKED ME PERSONALLY TO BRING YOU A MESSAGE IF ANY HARM SHOULD COME TO HIM ON THE NIGHT OF AUGUST 2ND.

YOU INTRIGUE ME... WHAT WAS THE MESSAGE?

"I AM A BAD LOSER."

IS THAT ALL?

NO, THERE WAS ALSO A POSTSCRIPT.

BANG

22

MODUS OPERANDI

GREEN MANOR CLUB, 16TH SEPTEMBER 1882.

THIS IS A DEPARTURE INTO RETIREMENT THAT HAS BEEN D...DESERVEDLY CELEBRATED!

YES, INDEED!

INSPECTOR GRAY? BEFORE LEAVING, I WOULD LIKE TO ASSURE YOU OF MY TOTAL ADMIRATION...

YOU REMAIN A ROLE MODEL FOR ALL THE INSPECTORS IN SCOTLAND YARD!

THANK YOU.

AFTER HAVING SOLVED ALL THE CASES ENTRUSTED TO YOU, YOU MUST BE LEAVING YOUR POST WITH A LIGHT HEART.

SPARE ME YOUR LITTLE PIECE. YOU KNOW PERFECTLY WELL THAT MY CAREER ENDED IN CHECKMATE.

OH, THE "JOHN SMITH" AFFAIR...

YES, THAT SERIAL KILLER WHO HAS COMMITTED TEN MURDERS IN THE COURSE OF THE LAST SIX MONTHS.

PERHAPS YOUR SUCCESSOR WILL FINALLY CATCH HIM!

I HAVE GRAVE DOUBTS...

I KNOW WHO JOHN SMITH IS.

AND NOBODY WILL EVER BE ABLE TO ARREST HIM...

WHEN THE FIRST MURDER TOOK PLACE, I THOUGHT IT WOULD ONLY TAKE A FEW WEEKS TO ARREST THE KILLER.

THIS GROSS WAY OF KILLING, THE LETTER LEFT AT THE SCENE OF THE CRIME ... ALL THIS DENOTING A CERTAIN CLUMSINESS ON THE PART OF THE CRIMINAL.

"I WILL KILL AGAIN," SIGNED "JOHN SMITH."

YOU SEE, A SERIAL KILLER IS ALWAYS TRACKED DOWN BY HIS "MODUS OPERANDI," HIS WAY OF OPERATING.

EACH NEW MURDER REVEALS HIS PERSONALITY A LITTLE MORE, AND THE DAY OF HIS ARREST DRAWS NEARER.

NOW, IT IS CERTAINLY TRUE THAT JOHN SMITH HAS BEEN CLEVERER THAN WE.

AT FIRST, HE WAITED PATIENTLY FOR THE FUSS TO DIE DOWN.

THEN, A YEAR TO THE DAY AFTER THE FIRST MURDER, HE STRUCK TWICE AT AN INTERVAL OF ONE HOUR.

BUT THIS TIME, JOHN SMITH HAD CHOSEN TWO DIFFERENT MODUS OPERANDI.

2

THE EXPERTS ON MENTAL ILLNESS COULDN'T MAKE HEAD OR TAIL OF IT.

HOW CAN WE DETERMINE THE PERSONALITY OF A KILLER WHO NEVER USES THE SAME METHOD TWICE?

BUT, FOR MY PART, I WAS PERSUADED THAT THE KILLER WAS NOT MAD AND THAT HE WAS DELIBERATELY CONFUSING THE TRAIL.

IN ORDER TO ARREST HIM, I HAD TO UNDERSTAND THE LOGIC OF THE APPARENT INCOHERENCE OF HIS MURDERS.

BUT JOHN SMITH DID NOT ACT WITH ANY LOGIC. HE KILLED RICH AND POOR, YOUNG AND OLD, WITH A KNIFE OR A REVOLVER.

MORE AND MORE HE SEEMED TO ME TO BE LIKE AN ELUSIVE AND MALICIOUS PHANTOM.

UNTIL THE DAY THAT JOHN SMITH LET ME KNOW THAT HE WAS READY TO MEET ME.

THIS REVELATION HELPED ME DISCOVER A COMMON FACTOR TO ALL THE MURDERS...

EACH WAS A CASE OF A CANTANKE-ROUS AUNT, A HATED NEIGHBOUR OR A TYRANNICAL FATHER. **NONE OF THE VICTIMS WAS MISSED BY THOSE CLOSEST TO HIM OR HER!**

THAT EVIDENCE SHOULD HAVE STRUCK ME BEFORE...BUT I WILL SAY IN MY DEFENCE THAT THESE DAYS THERE ARE RATHER MORE SINCERELY WEEPING LOVED ONES WHO MAKE THE EXCEPTION.

I WAS THEN CONVINCED THAT **JOHN SMITH HAD NEVER EXISTED!**

AT THE BEGINNING, HE HAD TO BE CREATED TO LEAD THE POLICE ON A FALSE TRAIL AND TO COVER UP A LOATHSOME MURDER.

THEN HIS VERY COMMON NAME INSPIRED MORE THAN ONE AMATEUR KILLER. THERE WERE EVEN TWO WHO HAD THE IDEA OF MAKING THEIR MARK ON THE "ANNIVERSARY" OF THE FIRST MURDER!

IT IS IN THIS WAY THAT ALL THE "SMALL MURDERERS" GATHERED THE COURAGE TO PASS FOR JOHN SMITH, AND IN SO DOING EMBODIED A MONSTER.

... AND SO HOW DO YOU ARREST A MURDERER WHO DOESN'T EXIST?

WHY HAVEN'T YOU TOLD ALL THIS TO THE PRESS?

THIS IS ONLY AN INTUITION: NONE OF THE VARIOUS MURDERERS LEFT ANY EVIDENCE...

...AND THEN PUBLIC OPINION DEMANDS A GUILTY PARTY, A **MONSTER THAT IT CAN HATE.** IT REFUSES TO BELIEVE IN A "COLLECTIVE KILLER" THAT MAKES IT FACE UP TO ITS RESPONSIBILITIES!

JOHN SMITH WILL CONTINUE TO KILL WITH IMPUNITY, BECAUSE THOSE WHO HAVE NEED OF HIS SERVICES ARE SO NUMEROUS.

I AM TIRED. I ASK YOU TO LEAVE ME ALONE FOR THE PRESENT.

OF COURSE, INSPECTOR GRAY.

OH!! YES, OF COURSE!!

GEORGE! BRING ME A SCOTCH!

I'M GOING TO START TOMORROW WITH THE **ARREST OF JOHN SMITH.**

MY FELICITATIONS, SIR.

29

6

HENRY, HAVE YOU SEEN THIS? THEY'VE ARRESTED JOHN SMITH!

WHAT?... THAT'S IMPOSSIBLE!

"SCANDAL IN SCOTLAND YARD! JOHN SMITH WAS NONE OTHER THAN INSPECTOR GRAY, THE POLICEMAN ENTRUSTED WITH THE ARREST OF THE MURDERER!"

HE WAS DENOUNCED BY AN ANONYMOUS LETTER AND HE HAS CONFESSED, IN WRITING AND IN DETAIL, TO ALL THE MURDERS HE HAS COMMITTED.

...

AN INSPECTOR! CAN YOU IMAGINE? THAT'S WHY THE KILLER HAS NEVER BEEN CAUGHT!

BESIDES, I HAVE ALWAYS... HENRY! ARE YOU LISTENING ?!

I AM SURE THAT HE SENT THE ANONYMOUS LETTER HIMSELF...

YES, DEAR.

THE OLD BRIGAND HAS FOUND A MEANS OF DELIVERING A CREDIBLE KILLER TO THE PUBLIC.

SO JOHN SMITH CANNOT CREATE ANY MORE VICTIMS.

YOU'RE STILL DAYDREAMING! MAMMA WARNED ME ABOUT THAT!

SCRATCH

SCRATCH SCRATCH SCRATCH

THE TRUTH IS THAT YOU ARE COMPLETELY USELESS!!

YES, DEAR.

21 HALBERDS

GREEN MANOR CLUB, MARCH 1893.

I ENTIRELY AGREE WITH THE AUTHOR DE QUINCY WHEN HE CONSIDERS ASSASSINATION TO BE ONE OF THE FINE ARTS.

...BUT IT MUST BE STATED THAT THIS ART LACKS A VERITABLE MASTERPIECE.

COME, DEAR FRIEND, IT SEEMS TO ME THAT HISTORY CONTAINS SEVERAL BRIGHT JEWELS OF THIS GENRE!

WAIT A MINUTE: WHAT ABOUT THE INCREDIBLE SELF-SINKING BOAT THAT NERO DEVISED TO KILL HIS MOTHER?

MUST I REMIND YOU THAT THE ATTEMPT RAN AGROUND?

AND COLIGNY? THROWN OUT OF THE WINDOW ON THE ORDERS OF THE DUKE OF GUISE IN THE MIDST OF THE SAINT BARTHOLOMEW'S DAY MASSACRE? ISN'T THAT EPIC STRUGGLE ENOUGH TO SEDUCE YOU?

TAKING ADVANTAGE OF A COLLECTIVE MASSACRE TO ACCOMPLISH A MURDER—THAT'S TOO EASY.

HOW ABOUT THE MURDER OF ABEL BY CAIN?

THE FIRST MURDERER, BUT TOO PRIMITIVE...NO, NO, THE ART OF MURDER STILL AWAITS ITS MASTERPIECE.

...AND IF, RATHER THAN WAIT PASSIVELY, WE TRY TO CARRY OUT SUCH A MASTERPIECE OURSELVES?

WELL, UPON MY WORD!

1

WE MUST CHOOSE CAREFULLY THE MOTIVE, THE VICTIM, THE WEAPON, AS WELL AS THE TIME AND PLACE OF THE CRIME SO THAT OUR MASTERPIECE IS A COMPLETE SUCCESS!

OUR MOTIVE WILL BE, PURELY AND SIMPLY, A LOVE OF THE ART.

IN FACT, NO PERSONAL ANTIPATHY MUST INTERFERE WITH OUR CHOICE OF VICTIM.

YES, EXACTLY! A PERSONAL MOTIVE WOULD BESMIRCH THE RIGOUR OF OUR PROCEEDINGS.

WE WILL CHOOSE, THUS, A PERSON FOR WHOM WE HAVE AFFECTION, EVEN ADMIRATION.

WHAT DO YOU SAY TO **CONAN DOYLE?**

THE CREATOR OF SHERLOCK HOLMES?! HE IS MY FAVOURITE AUTHOR!!

YES, WELL, ISN'T HE IN HIS WAY ONE OF THE MASTERS OF CRIME? TO IMPLICATE HIM IN OUR MASTER-PIECE WOULD BE A GOOD WAY OF PAYING HOMAGE!

DO YOU REMEMBER THE SUBTLE AND HORRIBLE MURDER THAT HE INVENTED IN "THE SPECKLED BAND"?

AH! SO SUBTLE AND SO HORRIBLE!

YES. MURDERING CONAN DOYLE, THAT WOULD BE GREAT, SERIOUS AND BEAUTIFUL!

I PROPOSE A TOAST TO HIM!

TO CONAN DOYLE!

2

IT IS ESSENTIAL TO MAKE A GOOD CHOICE FOR THE TIME AND PLACE OF THE CRIME.

WHO WOULD REMEMBER THE MURDER OF MARAT IF HE HAD BEEN KILLED AT NIGHT IN AN ALLEY?

BUT HE WAS STABBED IN THE DAYTIME IN HIS BATH, AND IT IS THIS THAT EXCITES INTEREST!

FOLLOW ME, DEAR FRIEND...

HAVE YOU GOT AN IDEA IN THE BACK OF YOUR MIND?

SUPPOSE CONAN DOYLE WERE INVITED TO TAKE PART IN A CONFERENCE, IN THE OPEN AIR AT THE FOOT OF THE CLOCK TOWER AT THE UNIVERSITY OF KINGSTON.

AND NOW IMAGINE IF HE WERE ASSASSINATED JUST AS THE BELL WAS STRIKING MIDDAY IN FRONT OF A STUPEFIED CROWD!

DING

DONG
DING

IMAGINE THE HEAVY TOLLING OF THE BELL MAKING A LUGUBRIOUS ECHO OF THE LAST BEATS OF THE VICTIM'S HEART...

GRANDIOSE! MAGNIFICENT!

DONG

DONG

WHAT'S MORE, MY POSITION AS DEAN OF THE UNIVERSITY WILL GREATLY FACILITATE THE ORGANISATION OF AN ASSASSINATION IN THE HEART OF THIS ANCIENT ESTABLISHMENT.

I'M GOING HOME FOR LUNCH. WHAT ABOUT MEETING TOMORROW EVENING AT EIGHT O'CLOCK TO CHOOSE THE WEAPON FOR THE CRIME?

VERY WELL.

THE TYPE OF WEAPON MUST FULLY PARTICIPATE IN THE DRAMATIC NATURE OF THE ASSASSINATION.

THAT'S WHY I THOUGHT OF THE HALBERD, AS IT IS A BAROQUE SYMBOL OF SOUND AND FURY!

GOOD THINKING!

TO TELL YOU THE TRUTH, I EVEN INTENDED TO USE 21 HALBERDS!

?! DON'T YOU FEAR THAT SUCH A NUMBER WOULD APPEAR... EXCESSIVE?

BUT TRUE ART DOES NOT ALLOW ITSELF TO BE TIMID IF IT IS GOING TO TRAVERSE THE CENTURIES! LET US NOT ERR THROUGH LACK OF AUDACITY!

CAESAR, WAS NOT HE STABBED 24 TIMES? WAS THAT NOT EXCESSIVE? AND YET WHAT A MEMORABLE MURDER!

SHHH!

SH!

YOU'RE RIGHT!!

SHHH!

WE ARTISTS DEMAND RESPECT!

LOUTS!

THAT'S EVERYTHING IN PLACE! WHEN THE BELL TOLLS MIDDAY, THIS HANDY MECHANISM WILL TIP UP THE HALBERDS, WHICH WILL SMASH THROUGH THE WINDOW...

KRRR

AT WHICH POINT A SHOWER OF GLASS AND STEEL WILL HIT THE UNFORTUNATE *CONAN DOYLE!*

ANY RISK OF FAILURE?

MY DEAR FRIEND! YOU ARE SPEAKING TO A MEMBER OF THE MILITARY ENGINEERS OF HER MOST GRACIOUS MAJESTY.

KRRR...

AND ON YOUR SIDE, ANY CHANCE THAT THE POLICE WILL CATCH UP WITH YOU?

NONE! WHAT INTEREST WOULD A DEAN HAVE IN RUINING THE REPUTATION OF HIS UNIVERSITY BY COMMITTING A MURDER?

KRRR..

... AND WHAT IS MORE, NOBODY ELSE KNOWS ABOUT THIS PASSAGE PERMITTING UNSEEN ACCESS TO THE CLOCK.

KRRR

KRR...

5

I HAVE NOW FINISHED MY BRIEF LECTURE ON CRIME STORIES. HAVE YOU ANY QUESTIONS?

YOU KNOW THAT 21 HALBERDS HAVE RECENTLY BEEN STOLEN FROM THE DUKE OF FOXWORD! WOULDN'T THAT BE A SOURCE OF INSPIRATION FOR THE NEXT STORY?

IT IS TRUE THAT I AM ALWAYS KEEN ON ELEMENTS THAT COULD NOURISH MY INTRIGUES...

...BUT TO UTILISE THIS PARTICULAR FACT IS A STEP THAT I WOULD NOT TAKE!

THE HALBERD IS AN **INCONGRUOUS** OBJECT, WITH ITS GREAT BIZARRE BLADE... HA! HA! HA!... **AND THOSE RIDICULOUS POMPOMS!!**

HA! HA! HA! HA! HA! HA!

HA! HA! HA! HA!
HA! HA! HA! HU!
HU! HU! HU! HU!
HU! HE! HE! HE!
HO! HO! HO!
HO! HO! HO!
HA! HA! HA!

AND TO MY EYES THE USE OF A HALBERD IN A CRIME STORY WOULD BE AN UNPARDONABLE BREACH OF TASTE.

HA! HA! HA!
HO! HO! HO!
HU! HU!
HA! HA! HA!
HA! HA!
HA! HA!
HA! HA!
HA! HA! HA!

HA! HA! HA!
PARDON! EXCUSE ME!
SORRY!
HA! HA! HA!
HO! HO! HO!
HA! HA!
HU! HU!
HA! HA!
HA! HA! HA!
HA! HA!

PUFF!

PUFF!

QUICK! WE HAVE ONLY A FEW SECONDS TO AVOID THE IRREPARABLE!!

SUTTER 1801

GREEN MANOR CLUB, APRIL 1872.

THIS PAINTING BELONGED TO LORD DENTON. WE VALUE IT HIGHLY.

IT WAS A LITTLE DAMAGED AT THE TIME OF THE FIRE LAST YEAR. I AM CONFIDENT THAT YOUR TALENTS AS A RESTORER WILL BRING IT BACK TO ITS FORMER GLORY.

THE WORK MADE ME ILL AT EASE AT FIRST GLANCE...

"JASON SUTTER... BORN IN 1779 IN EDINBURGH... SELF-TAUGHT GENIUS... INFLUENCED BY WORK OF FUSELI."

"INVITED TO ABE'S MANOR BY LORD DENTON, HE PAINTS A 'PORTRAIT OF THE FAMILY,' WHICH WOULD BE HIS LAST WORK."

"HIS SUICIDE AT THE AGE OF 22 YEARS DEPRIVED ENGLAND OF AN ARTIST WHO SEEMED DESTINED TO BECOME ONE OF THE GREAT PORTRAITISTS OF THE 19TH CENTURY."

IT TOOK ME SEVERAL DAYS TO UNDERSTAND MY PROBLEM WITH THE PICTURE.

THE LINES OF CONSTRUCTION... THE LINES OF PERSPECTIVE...

THE TERRIFIED LOOK OF THE HORSE IN THE BACKGROUND.

ALL CONVERGED TOWARDS THE EYE OF LORD DENTON, GIVING THE SINISTER IMPRESSION THAT THIS PERSONAGE WITH THE INSCRUTABLE EXPRESSION WAS THE CENTRE OF EVERYTHING.

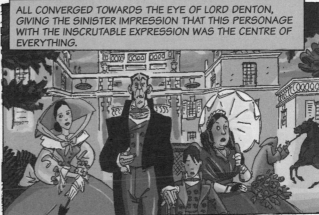

BUT ANOTHER DETAIL INTRIGUED ME.

THE SLEEVE OF THE GROOM WITH THE VARIEGATED COLOURS DID NOT SEEM TO CONFORM TO THE TRADITIONAL COSTUME OF A SERVANT.

IN FACT, ONE WOULD HAVE SAID THAT THE COSTUME WAS THAT OF A "HARLE-QUIN," ONE OF THOSE BUFFOONS WHO AMUSE THE PUBLIC AT THE THEATRE.

THE THEATRE! YES, THAT WAS ONE OF THE CLUES TO THE PICTURE!

2

EVERYTHING IN THE PICTURE COMBINED TO GIVE THE IMPRESSION OF A PLAY: EVEN THE TREES, LIKE CURTAINS FRAMING THE SCENE.

OR THE PERSONAGES, LIT AS IF BY CANDLES! SUTTER SEEMED TO BE ILLUSTRATING THE WORDS OF PETRONIUS: "ALL THE WORLD PLAYS COMEDY"...

BUT WAS IT A MATTER OF A GENERAL VISION OF THE WORLD, OR OF A PRECISE ACCUSATION AIMED AT THE DENTONS?

BECAUSE AN ATTENTIVE STUDY OF THE PICTURE HAD REVEALED TO ME A TROUBLING DETAIL.

ONE RETOUCH, WHICH WAS CLEARLY NOT DONE BY THE YOUNG PAINTER...

...AND WHICH HAD SERVED TO MASK SOME TOUCHES OF RED THAT SUTTER HAD GIVEN TO ONE OF THE WALLS OF THE MANOR.

SO, YOU WISH TO GO TO ABE'S MANOR...

FOR AS LONG AS IT TAKES TO MAKE SOME ROUGH SKETCHES OF THE BUILDING. THAT WILL FACILITATE MY WORK.

VERY WELL, IF IT IS REALLY NECESSARY... JOSEPH WILL TAKE YOU THERE.

SUTTER MUST HAVE STAYED IN THIS SECONDARY HOUSE. NO DOUBT HE DID NOT HAVE THE RIGHT TO STAY IN THE PRINCIPAL RESIDENCE.

THE DAUGHTER OF LORD DENTON.

Sutter 1800

SHE IS BEAUTIFUL, ISN'T SHE?

THE POOR YOUNG LADY DIED SO YOUNG... FOLLOWING A LONG ILLNESS, IT SEEMS, HARDLY A YEAR AFTER THIS PICTURE WAS PAINTED.

IT WAS A GREAT GRIEF TO HER FATHER. THEY SAY HE ADORED HER!

4

THERE WAS STILL ONE THING FOR ME TO CHECK.

HERE... THIS IS THE AREA THAT HAD THE TOUCHES OF RED SHOWN BY SUTTER IN THE PICTURE.

YES, THE STONE IS MORE FRIABLE. THIS MUST BE A SMALL BASEMENT WINDOW, WHICH HAS BEEN WALLED UP.

I REMEMBER HAVING THE EXCITED FEELING OF BEING ABLE AT LAST TO CROSS THE SURFACE OF THE PICTURE...

MY GOD!

I MUST GO TO LONDON IMMEDIATELY.

I HAD TO TRY AND SORT OUT MY THOUGHTS AND TO PIECE TOGE-THER THE CHAIN OF TERRIBLE EVENTS THAT HAD TAKEN PLACE AT ABE'S MANOR.

THE PASSION ARISING BETWEEN THE PAINTER AND HIS MODEL.

...A POSSESSIVE AND TYRANNICAL FATHER, DRIVEN VIOLENTLY MAD BY THE IDEA OF SEEING HIS DAUGHTER IN LOVE WITH THIS ARTIST.

A SECOND ORDER BY WAY OF A TRAP ...

BECAUSE, ONCE THE PAINTER WAS INSTALLED AT ABE'S MANOR, HE WAS FORBIDDEN TO SEE MARY. HE WAS REDUCED TO REPRODUCING, BRUSH STROKE BY BRUSH STROKE, THE PRECEDING PORTRAIT.

THE MANOR AND ITS INHABITANTS SEEMED TO BE HELD UNDER A CLOAK OF LIES AND FALSE PRETENCES.

PLAYING CAT AND MOUSE, DID LORD DENTON FINALLY MAKE HIM UNDERSTAND BY DROPPING HINTS AS TO WHERE MARY WAS?

...THAT SHE WAS VERY NEAR, SHUT IN BEHIND A WALL, AND FOREVER INACCESSIBLE TO THE PAINTER?

BEFORE FORCING HIM TO "SUICIDE," DID HE REVEAL WHAT I MYSELF FINALLY DISCOVERED?...

THAT THE YOUNG GIRL HAD BEEN WALLED UP?

MY GOD!

... SO MANY ELEMENTS THAT I ALONE COULD NOT THROW LIGHT ON.

TAKE ME TO SCOTLAND YARD!

6.

THE CLUB? BUT...

PLEASE FOLLOW ME, SIR.

MY DEAR FRIEND! I ASKED JOSEPH TO BRING YOU HERE ON YOUR RETURN FROM ABE'S MANOR.

YOUR WORK UP TO THE PRESENT HAS BEEN EXTREMELY SATISFACTORY. YOU ARE TALENTED. BESIDES, I BELIEVE THAT YOU ARE DESTINED FOR A PAINTING CAREER, ISN'T THAT RIGHT?

WHEN YOU HAVE FINISHED YOUR WORK ON THE PAINTING, WOULD IT PLEASE YOU TO STUDY IN ROME? I HAVE SOME CONTACTS IN THE MEDICI VILLA. I COULD PAY FOR YOUR STAY...JUST LIKE MY GRANDFATHER, LORD DENTON, I AM A PATRON OF THE ARTS.

CRUNCH CRUNCH

HE KNEW THAT I KNEW, AND HE WAS MAKING ME A PROPOSITION THAT I COULD NOT REFUSE.

IN THAT INSTANT I UNDERSTOOD THE SIGNIFICANCE OF THE ENIGMATIC EXPRESSION OF LORD DENTON...IT WAS A COMPLICIT LOOK.

BUT I HAVE DECIDED TO FIGHT IN MY OWN WAY...MY PAINTING WILL BE MY REVENGE.

REMEMBER MY NAME, ERIC KAYE. SOON IT WILL SHINE BRIGHTLY IN THE FIRMAMENT OF THE CENTURY.

I MUST DO IT FOR SUTTER.

7

Green MANOR

THE BALLAD OF DR. THOMPSON

1878, GREEN MANOR CLUB, TWO O'CLOCK IN THE MORNING.

TAKE CARE, GENTLEMEN, THE ICE HAS MADE THE STEPS SLIPPERY.

DID YOU HEAR THAT, DOCTOR? DO YOU THINK YOU ARE CAPABLE OF DESCENDING THE STEPS?

HA! HA! LISTEN TO THE G... GOOD PROFESSOR BRIGHT WHO IS GIVING ME A LESSON!

ADMIT IT! YOU ARE JUST AS D... DRUNK AS I. YES!

EVEN IF I AM, I KEEP MY WITS ABOUT ME, SIR!

COACH-MAN!

HO, HO, YOU ARE DEFINITELY A VERY PRETENTIOUS PERSON! I UNDERSTAND A LITTLE BETTER EACH DAY WHY IT WAS I THAT MARGIE FINALLY MARRIED!

YOU DON'T DESERVE HER, YOU BLITHERING IDIOT!

I WILL LEAVE YOU NOW, YOU RAT! I'M GOING TO WALK HOME. THAT WILL CLEAR MY HEAD A BIT.

CUT THROUGH BY HILL STREET, YOU POOR SOT. YOU WILL GET BACK QUICKER TO YOUR CHARMING WIFE.

GOOD NIGHT, SCOUNDREL!

UNTIL TOMORROW, IMBECILE!

PROFESSOR, MY GOD! MY GOD! WAKE UP! THE POLICE ARE HERE...

MMM?...

THEY...THEY WANT TO ARREST YOU FOR THE MURDER OF DR. THOMPSON!

?!?

I KNOW YOU ARE GUILTY. WHAT I WANT TO UNDERSTAND IS WHY YOU HAVE CREATED THE CRAZY SCENE OF THE CRIME AROUND THE CORPSE OF DR. THOMPSON.

BUT WHAT DOES ALL THIS MEAN? WHAT HAS HAPPENED TO MY FRIEND?

I WILL REFRESH YOUR MEMORY, PROFESSOR BRIGHT!

THIS MORNING, ABOUT 6 O'CLOCK, TWO POLICE OFFICERS MADE A STRANGE DISCOVERY IN THE MIDDLE OF ELDER STREET.

BY JOVE!

THE CORPSE OF DR. THOMPSON IN A CLOCK!?

DON'T FAKE ASTONISHMENT; IT IS YOU WHO KILLED HIM!

ALL LONDON KNOWS THAT YOU WERE IN LOVE WITH MARGIE STEWART BEFORE SHE MARRIED THOMPSON! THE COACHMAN HEARD YOU QUARRELLING ON THIS SUBJECT IN FRONT OF THE CLUB.

BUT WE WERE DRUNK! WE QUARREL WITH EACH OTHER AS A SORT OF JOKE!!

AS FOR MARGIE, YES, I LOVED HER UNTIL I ACCEPTED THAT SHE HAD MARRIED ANOTHER WHO WAS MY BEST FRIEND, AS THEIR MUTUAL HAPPINESS DEPENDED ON IT.

NO DOUBT THIS IS BEYOND THE LIMITS OF YOUR IMAGINATION, INSPECTOR.

INSPECTOR, SIR?

AH! YOU HAVE FINISHED INTERROGATING THE WITNESSES?

THE DRIVER OF THE COACH DROPPED THE PROFESSOR AT THUMB'S PUBLIC HOUSE, WHERE HE PLAYED CARDS WITH HIS FRIENDS UNTIL SEVEN IN THE MORNING. IT WOULD SEEM, THEREFORE, IMPOSSIBLE FOR HIM TO HAVE...

THE DRIVER IS LYING!

THEN, WHY WOULD HE HAVE REPORTED THAT I HAD A QUARREL WITH THE DOCTOR?...

WELL, THEN, YOU ORDERED THE MURDER!

ADMIT, INSPECTOR, THAT YOU ARE FOLLOWING YOUR INSTINCT BUT YOU HAVE NO PROOF AGAINST ME.

BECAUSE I AM NOT THE MURDERER OF MY FRIEND, AND TO PROVE IT, I AM GOING TO HELP YOU LAY HANDS ON THE TRUE GUILTY PARTIES.

IN THE FACE OF THIS EXTRAORDINARY SITUATION, ONE CAN NO LONGER RELY ON INSTINCT BUT ON THE POWERS OF ANALYSIS: ASK YOURSELF FOR WHAT VALID REASON WOULD THE CRIMINALS LEAVE THE BODY IN THE MIDDLE OF THE STREET...

FOR A CHALLENGE? UNLIKELY. THEY WOULD HAVE CHOSEN A MORE CONSPICUOUS PLACE.

ONE CAN, ON THE OTHER HAND, IMAGINE THAT, SEEING A POLICE PATROL COMING, THEY WERE FORCED TO ABANDON THEIR LOAD IN THE STREET IN ORDER TO RUN AWAY...

RANSPORT ODY IN A LOCK?

THAT IS INDEED THE SECOND QUESTION TO ASK...

IT WAS THE ONLY THING THEY COULD FIND IN WHICH TO HIDE THE BODY, AND THEY WERE AMATEURS!

...AND IT SEEMS TO ME THAT THEY WERE MAKING FOR THE THAMES TO JETTISON THEIR SINISTER CARGO...

GOOD HEA-VENS!

THE STREET WHERE THE BODY WAS FOUND IS MIDWAY BETWEEN THE RIVER AND THE SLUMS OF HAMILTON STREET. SEE IF ANY FAMILY HAS "LOST" ITS CLOCK.

LATER...

HERE THEY ARE.

IT'S NOT OUR FAULT!

IT'S THE FAULT OF THE OLD MAN!

EXPLAIN YOURSELF.

THE OLD MAN BROUGHT THE CORPSE IN HIS CART.

IT COULD HARDLY BE LEFT LYING ON THE PAVEMENT!

UH, HUH.

AND AS JAMES WAS COMING OUT OF PRISON, WE WANTED TO GET RID OF THE BODY SO THE POLICE WOULD NOT THINK THAT ...

UH, HUH.

SO, THAT WAS A COMPLETE WASHOUT!

4

51

SIR, WHERE DID YOU FIND THE BODY?

IN KENNETH STREET...

I WAS COLLECTING WOOD WHEN I HEARD THESE U...

THEY WERE DANCING AROUND THE BODY.

WHEN THEY SAW ME, THEY LEGGED IT! BUT I RECOGNISED LITTLE MATTHEW. HE IS A GOOD-FOR-NOTHING!!

I KNOW HIM.

THE DOCTOR'S BRIEFCASE WAS FOUND ON YOU...

IT'S NOT MY FAULT, SIR.

TELL US HOW YOU CAME TO HAVE THE BRIEFCASE...

WELL, THIS BLOKE WAS DEAD, SO OBVIOUSLY HE DIDN'T NEED IT.

AND WHY WERE YOU DANCING AROUND THE BODY?

IT'S JUST SOMETHING WE DO WHEN WE FIND EASY MONEY.

DID YOU AND YOUR GANG KILL THE DOCTOR?

NO, I SWEAR! THE BLOKE WAS ALREADY DEAD WHEN HE WAS FOUND IN THE TREE!

5

THIS DIRTY LITTLE BASTARD IS MAKING FUN OF US!

HE WOULDN'T INVENT SUCH A STORY. WE MUST USE OUR POWERS OF ANALYSIS AGAIN.

THE DOCTOR HAD NO REASON TO CLIMB INTO A TREE, AND IT WOULD APPEAR TO BE DIFFICULT AND POINTLESS FOR CRIMINALS TO HANG UP HIS BODY IN THE BRANCHES...

...THEN, PERHAPS HE FELL! YES, THAT WOULD BE LOGICAL.

WHAT?

KENNETH STREET IS FULL OF OVERHANGING ROOFS. HAVE A LOOK TO SEE WHERE THE BODY COULD HAVE FALLEN FROM!

THE NEXT MORNING...

YOU WERE RIGHT. THE BODY FELL FROM 34 MILLER STREET, 5TH FLOOR.

IT WAS A CERTAIN BILLY WHO FOUND HIM IN THE STREET, REEKING OF ALCOHOL. HE DID NOT WANT TO LEAVE HIM THERE OUTSIDE IN THE COLD.

SO HE TOOK HIM HOME.

AND HE CLAIMS THAT HE AND THE DRUNK PARTED COMPANY WHILE HE WAS SEARCHING FOR HIS KEYS.

6

SO THAT IS HOW THOMPSON DIED. WHAT A STRANGE BALLAD IT WOULD MAKE...

ONE LAST DETAIL, HOWEVER.

THE AUTOPSY HAS RE... HE WAS ALREADY DEA... BILLY FOUND HIM AT THE... THE STAIRS IN HILL STR...

IT WAS FREEZING THAT NIGHT, AND THE STEPS OF THIS ALLEYWAY ARE VERY STEEP. THOMPSON BEING FULL UP WITH DRINK, A FALL WAS PREDICTABLE...

... ESPECIALLY FOR A SHARP MIND LIKE YOURS, PROFESSOR. YOUR COACH-MAN TOLD ME THAT YOU ADVISED THE DOCTOR TO CUT THROUGH BY THIS ALLEY...YOU ARE UNDER ARREST.

... NOW, YES... I REMEMBER THE FLEETING AND TERRIBLE HATRED THAT I FELT FOR THOMPSON THAT EVENING, WHEN HE SPOKE OF MARGIE...

IT IS POSSIBLE THAT I WOULD HAVE WISHED HIS DEATH TO THE POINT OF INCITING HIM TO GO BY THE ALLEY WHEN I KNEW VERY WELL THAT IT WAS DANGEROUS?

I WAS DRUNK... AND NOW I DON'T REMEMBER VERY WELL... BUT I DON'T WANT TO REMEMBER...

GOD! IS IT POSSIBLE THAT ALL THIS TIME I HAVE BEEN ENQUIRING INTO A MURDER THAT I MYSELF COMMITTED?

I KNEW IT FROM THE START...

... MY INSTINCT NEVER FAILS ME.